G000135309

Three Adventures of Sherlock Holmes

Sir Arthur Conan Doyle

Simplified by Frances Johnston

Longman

Longman Group UK Limited,
Longman House, Burnt Mill, Harlow,
Essex CM20 2JE, England
and Associated Companies throughout the world.

This simplified edition © Longman Group UK Limited 1987

First published 1987
Sixth impression 1991

ISBN 0-582-52286-2

Set in 10/13 point Linotron 202 Versailles
Produced by Longman Group (FE) Limited
Printed in Hong Kong

Acknowledgements

'Photographs © BBC' 1968 for page 39; Photographs from THE
ADVENTURES OF SHERLOCK HOLMES, COURTESY GRANADA
TELEVISION' for pages 7 and 18; TV Times/Transworld Feature
Syndicate (UK) Ltd for pages 27, 31, 47 and the cover.

The cover background is a wallpaper design called NUAGE,
courtesy of Osborne and Little plc.

Stage 4: 1800 word vocabulary

Please look under *New words* at the back of this book
for explanations of words outside this stage.

Contents

Introduction

Sir Arthur Conan Doyle

Conan Doyle, born in 1859, was a doctor of medicine. He had a very keen mind, rather like that of his most famous character, Sherlock Holmes. Doyle's first story about Holmes, *A Study in Scarlet*, appeared in a magazine in 1887.

After 1890, Conan Doyle stopped practising medicine and became a full-time writer. More and more Sherlock Holmes stories appeared in magazines and were collected in books like *The Memoirs of Sherlock Holmes* (1894). Sherlock Holmes was also the subject of four full-length novels. The best-known of these is probably *The Hound of the Baskervilles* (1902), which has been made into films and television stories several times.

Perhaps the character, Sherlock Holmes, developed over the years, but from the beginning the detective had unusual powers of reasoning and deduction. There are examples in this book. In *The Speckled Band* Holmes deduces that danger will come through a ventilator and down a bell rope. In *The Five Orange Pips* he deduces that the murderers are on a sailing ship, and he finds the actual ship by reasoning from sailing dates. In *The Crown of Diamonds*, Holmes's powers of deduction lead him to the man who has the missing diamonds, and to an understanding of the behaviour of the innocent son.

Holmes's friend, Doctor Watson, is not a fool (though some films have made him seem foolish), but he is an ordinary man without Holmes's special powers of mind.

He is a brave man, and is often able to help the detective in moments of danger. We find ourselves seeing the action through Watson's eyes, and indeed in very many of Holmes's cases – two in this book – Watson tells the story, and so we receive the explanations that Watson himself needs.

In a number of his cases – but not in the three stories in this book – Holmes's great enemy was the master criminal Moriarty. When Conan Doyle decided that he had written enough Sherlock Holmes stories, he wrote one in which, in finally defeating the evil Moriarty, the great detective lost his own life. There was a public outcry. Doyle's readers were quite angry, and he had to write a story in which Holmes appeared again. He hadn't died after all!

When Conan Doyle tried to kill Sherlock Holmes, it was because he wanted to spend his time on his more "serious" writing. This included some historical novels, for example, *The White Company* (1890), *Rodney Stone* (1896), and *Sir Nigel* (1906).

But it is for Sherlock Holmes that Conan Doyle is remembered, and not for his historical novels or his works arising from his belief in spiritualism (messages to living people from dead people).

Modern detective stories usually deal with murder. Although there are murders in two of the stories in this book, Sherlock Holmes's cases do not necessarily include murder. In some cases there is not even a crime, because Sherlock Holmes has prevented the crime.

Many modern writers seem to consider that the most important thing about a detective story is a detective. Conan Doyle knew that much greater importance must be given to the story, and that the reader must feel that he or she is present as the story unfolds.

The three stories
The Speckled Band, The Five Orange Pips and *The Crown of Diamonds* were all written at about the same time, between 1890 and 1905. We can learn from them about the way of life in England at that time.

People travelled by steamships and steam trains, and steamships are important in the story of *The Five Orange Pips*. There was a good service of steam trains to such places as Horsham and Streatham, mentioned in these stories. The underground railways of London began with steam trains in 1863; the electric trains of the "Twopenny tube" (two pence to any station) ran in tunnels from 1900, but one doesn't read much about them in Conan Doyle's stories. The telephone was invented in 1876, but telephones were not common; Holmes uses the very good postal and telegraph services. The bell rope in *The Speckled Band* ought to have worked a set of wires passing over pulley wheels to ring a bell in the kitchen mechanically, but it was false. The lamps in that story are oil lamps.

The Speckled Band

Chapter 1

The problem of the speckled band was one of the first in which I, Dr Watson, was able to help my friend Sherlock Holmes.

It was a long time ago, when Holmes and I were sharing rooms in Baker Street. At the time, I promised to keep everything a secret. But the lady is now dead, and perhaps it is right for people to know the truth.

It was early in April of 1883 that I was suddenly awakened to find Sherlock Holmes standing by my bed.

I looked at him in surprise. It was only seven o'clock.

"Very sorry to wake you, Watson," he said.

"What is it, then? A fire?"

"No. A young lady has arrived. She seems very unhappy, and wants to see me. Now, if young ladies wander about London at this early hour, I imagine that they want to talk about something very important. I thought that you might like to help me in this case, so you should come now to hear what she has to say."

"My dear fellow, I wouldn't miss it for anything."

My greatest pleasure was to help Holmes in his detective work, and during the last eight years I have watched him in more than seventy cases. Working, as he always did, for the love of his art, and not for wealth, he only accepted cases that interested him.

I dressed quickly, and was ready in a few minutes, and followed Holmes down to the sitting room.

Chapter 2

A lady dressed in black, wearing a thick veil, was sitting by the window. She stood up as we came into the room.

"Good morning, madam," said Holmes. "My name is Sherlock Holmes. This is my friend Dr Watson. You may say anything you wish to us, and know that we shall keep all we hear quite secret. I see that you are shaking. Please sit close to the fire and I shall order you a cup of coffee."

"It isn't the cold that makes me shake," said the woman quietly. "It's fear, Mr Holmes. It's terror!" She raised her veil then, and we saw that it was quite true. Her face was pale, her eyes were frightened, like those of some hunted animal. She looked about thirty years old, but her hair was already nearly white.

"You mustn't be afraid," said Holmes gently. He leaned forward to pat her arm. "We shall soon put matters right, I have no doubt."

"Sir, I shall go mad unless I can get help. I have heard of you; you helped a friend of mine when she badly needed it. Oh sir, do you think that you could help me too, and at least throw a little light through the darkness which is all round me? I can't pay you very much just now, but in a month or two I shall be married, and shall have my own money, if you will wait until then."

"I shall be happy to do my best for you, madam. As for paying, you may do that when it pleases you. Now you must tell me what is troubling you so much."

"Oh dear!" our visitor replied. "It's difficult to tell you anything that will be of any help to you. All the facts I have collected are so small and so unimportant, you might think it is all the imagination of a frightened woman."

"Tell me all you know, madam, and tell me about your family."

Chapter 3

"My name is Helen Stoner. I live with my stepfather, who is the last of a very famous family in England: the Roylotts of Stoke Moran in Surrey."

Holmes said, "Yes. I have heard the name."

"The family was once the richest in England with very large amounts of land extending into Berkshire in the north and Hampshire in the west.

"In the last hundred years the eldest sons have wasted the fortunes of the family until now nothing is left but a small piece of land and the old house, two hundred years old. A great deal of money was owed. The present eldest son, knowing that he had to make a living, became a doctor, and went to India. He was successful there until a great misfortune came to him. A thief broke into his house and stole many things, and in a fit of anger he blamed his servant and beat him so hard that the poor man died.

"Dr Roylott was sent to prison for many years for this terrible act, and after this he returned to England, a very disappointed and angry man.

"When Dr Roylott was in India, he married my mother, whose husband, my father, had died. My sister and I were twins and we were only two years old when my mother married again. She died eight years ago. She left Dr Roylott, our stepfather, all her money, but she ordered that when we got married he should provide us each with a certain amount of money every year.

"The money she left was enough for all our needs; there was every reason for us to live happily.

"But a terrible change came over our stepfather. He would not make friends with our neighbours. At first they had been glad to see the house at Stoke Moran once more occupied. But he shut himself in the house, and when he

3

did appear, quarrelled with everyone he saw. He became the terror of the village and people kept out of his way. They were afraid of his anger, because he was a strong man, and they knew what he had done to his servant in India. He also keeps snakes and other animals which he brought from India with him. He allows these creatures to go anywhere in the house and garden, frightening everybody."

Chapter 4

Helen Stoner went on with her story.

"You can imagine from all I say that my poor sister Julia and I did not have much pleasure in our lives.

"No servant ever stayed for long, and we did all the work in the house. She was only thirty years old when she died, and yet her hair was turning white, just as mine has done."

Holmes said, "Your sister is dead?"

"She died two years ago. That is why I have come to you.

"We were staying with a relation in London at Christmas time two years ago. There my sister met a man who asked her to marry him.

"When we returned to Stoke Moran, our stepfather seemed quite glad about the marriage. But two weeks before the wedding day a terrible thing happened."

Holmes was leaning back in his chair with his eyes closed, but at these words, he opened his eyes.

"Please tell me everything that happened that day."

"I can do that easily because every event of that terrible day is for ever in my memory.

"First I must explain to you the plan of the house. All our bedrooms are on the ground floor. First is Dr

Roylott's, the second was my sister's and the third is mine. They all open out into the same passage.

"The windows of these three rooms open out on the garden. The night of my sister's death, Dr Roylott had gone to his room early. Later we went to our bedrooms, but my sister came into my room.

"'I can't sleep,' she said. 'He's smoking, and the smell of those cigarettes is coming through to my room.'

"So we sat and talked until about eleven o'clock.

"When she got up to go, Julia paused at the door of my room.

"'Tell me, Helen,' she said, 'have you ever heard anyone whistling late at night?'

"'Never,' I said.

"'I suppose it is not you whistling in your sleep?'

"'No, certainly not. But why?'

"'Well, for the last few nights at about three in the morning I have heard a low, clear whistle. It always wakes me. I can't tell where it comes from, perhaps from the next room, perhaps from the garden. But I am surprised *you* don't hear it.'

"'I think I sleep more heavily than you do.'

"'Well, it doesn't matter,' she said, and she smiled at me and left the room, and a few minutes later I heard her lock her door."

"Indeed," said Holmes. "Was it your custom always to lock yourselves in at night?"

"Always."

"And why?"

"I think I told you that the doctor kept wild animals and a monkey that ran about at night. We did not feel safe unless our doors were locked."

"I understand. Please go on."

Chapter 5

Helen went on with her story. "I couldn't sleep that night. There was a storm. The wind was howling outside and the rain was beating against the windows.

"Suddenly I heard the wild scream of a terrified woman. I knew it was my sister's voice. I sprang from my bed and rushed into the passage. As I opened my door, I seemed to hear a low whistle, such as my sister described, and a second later a noise of metal falling.

"As I ran down the passage my sister's door was unlocked and I saw her appear, her face pale with terror, her hands stretched out for help. Her whole body was moving to and fro as if she was drunk.

"I ran to her and threw my arms round her, but her knees gave way and she fell to the ground. She seemed in terrible pain.

"'Oh, my God! Helen,' she whispered. 'It was the band! The speckled band!' She pointed in the direction of the doctor's room, but could say no more.

"By this time the doctor was coming out of his room. Both of us tried hard to save her life, but it was too late, and she died almost at once."

"One moment," said Holmes. "Are you sure about this whistle, and the noise of the metal falling? Are you quite certain about it?"

"I thought I heard it. The noise of the storm might have made me imagine it."

"Was your sister dressed?"

"No. She was in her nightclothes. In her right hand there was a burnt match and she had a match box in her left hand."

"Showing that she had struck a light and looked about her when first alarmed. That is important," said Holmes.

Helen Stoner hears her sister's screams

"The case was looked into with great care by the police. (Dr Roylott was not liked by most people because of his past.) But no one found any cause of the death. No one could have got into her room, so it is certain that my sister was quite alone when she met her death."

"There was no poison?"

"She was examined, but nothing was found."

"What do you think this unfortunate lady died of, then?" Holmes asked.

"I believe that she died of fear and great terror, though I cannot imagine what frightened her."

"Ah! And what did you think she meant by a band – a speckled band?"

"Perhaps some band of people, perhaps she was talking about gypsies – many of them wear handkerchiefs with spots on them, over their heads."

Holmes shook his head and looked very doubtful. "I don't know. I don't know. It is all very puzzling. But please go on with your story."

"Two years have passed since then. I am very much alone. However, last month, a dear friend whom I have known for many years asked me to marry him. His name is Percy Armitage. My stepfather has agreed to our marriage.

"Two days ago, my stepfather asked me to move into my sister's bedroom while some repairs are done to my room. So I had to sleep in her bed.

"Imagine, then, my terror when last night, as I lay awake, I suddenly heard the low whistle which she heard on the night she died. I sprang up and lit the lamp, but I could see nothing. I was too frightened to go to sleep again, so as soon as daylight came, I ran to the Crown Inn, which is quite near, and got a carriage to take me to the railway station, and so to you to ask your advice."

Chapter 6

"You have done wisely," said Holmes, "but have you told me everything?"

"Yes, everything."

"Miss Stoner, you have not. You are protecting your stepfather for some reason."

"Why, what do you mean?"

Instead of answering, Holmes picked up Helen Stoner's hand. On her arm, the marks of four fingers were red on the white skin.

"He's unkind to you," said Holmes.

The lady looked very unhappy. She covered her arm with her coat.

"He's a hard man," she said. "He doesn't know how strong he is."

There was a long silence, and Holmes stared into the fire. He spoke at last.

"This is a very deep business. There is so much more I want to know before I can act. Yet we mustn't waste any time. Is it possible for us to come to Stoke Moran today, and see these bedrooms, without the doctor knowing we are there?"

"Yes it is, because he is coming to London today. He will be away all day. Nothing will disturb you."

"Excellent. You will come with me, Watson?"

"I shall be very pleased to come."

"And Miss Stoner – what are your plans?"

"I shall return to Stoke Moran this morning, and I shall meet you when you arrive. So now I will go. My heart is lighter already since I have talked to you. I shall look forward to seeing you this afternoon."

She dropped her thick black veil over her face again and left the room.

Chapter 7

"And what do you think of it all, Watson?" asked Sherlock Holmes.

"It seems to me to be a very bad sort of case," I said. "We have the fact that, when the girls marry, Dr Roylott has to give them money. Perhaps that is enough to make a man do murder?"

"Perhaps. And that is why I want to go to Stoke Moran today. But what on earth——!" Holmes cried suddenly, as the door was thrown open, and a huge man appeared in the room.

"Which of you is Holmes?" said this man.

"That is my name, sir," said Holmes, "and will you be so kind as to tell me who you are."

"I am Dr Roylott of Stoke Moran."

"Indeed," said Holmes quietly. "Please sit down."

"No, I will not. My daughter has been here – what has she been telling you?"

"I find the weather a little cold today," said Holmes.

"What has she been saying to you?" shouted the doctor.

"But the flowers are starting to grow," continued Holmes.

"Ha! – I know you, you trouble maker! I have heard of you before now. You are Holmes, the man who pretends to be a policeman, who goes about making trouble for people."

Holmes laughed quietly. But all he said was, "When you go out, will you close the door, it's getting cold in here."

"You had better leave me alone. I am a dangerous man. I know that Miss Stoner has been here." And he left the room quickly.

"I do hope he won't attack Miss Stoner," I said.

"There is certainly no time to waste," said Holmes. "But before we go to Stoke Moran, I think I must try to find out more about this man. I'll go to the records office and try to get some help in this matter."

Chapter 8

It was nearly one o'clock when Sherlock Holmes returned. He held in his hand a piece of paper full of notes and figures.

"I have seen the will of the doctor's wife who died eight years ago. Certainly if the daughters marry, they can ask for nearly all the money that the doctor has. It is easy to see that he would be left with very little to live on."

"So," I said, "your morning's work has not been wasted. You have proved that the doctor has every reason to stop the young ladies from ever marrying."

"Yes," said Holmes. "And now the old man knows we are interested in him, so I think we should go at once to Stoke Moran. I would like you to have your pistol with you, Watson – and a toothbrush, because we may stay the night."

Miss Stoner was waiting for us when we arrived.

"Good afternoon, madam. You see we are here as we promised to be."

"I have been waiting so eagerly for you," she said, shaking hands with us warmly. "And isn't it splendid, Dr Roylott has gone to London and won't be back until late this evening."

"We have already met the doctor," said Holmes. "I am afraid he followed you to my house. He was very rude and very angry when I would not tell him why you had come to see me."

11

Miss Stoner turned very white as she listened.

"I never know when I am safe from him. What will he say when he returns home?"

"You must lock yourself away from him tonight. But first, please take me to see the bedrooms."

Chapter 9

Holmes looked at the three bedrooms.

"This one is yours, Miss Stoner? But I do not see that it is necessary for any repairs to be done."

"I think it is just to get me out of my room, and into my sister's room."

"It sounds very possible," said Holmes. He looked carefully at the doors. "As you both locked your rooms at night, no one could get in from the passage."

Next we locked the windows, and Holmes went outside into the garden and tried to force his way in, but without success. "Ha!" he said. "No one could get through these windows if they were shut. I think we must look inside the house for the guilty one."

We went back into the bedroom where Miss Stoner's poor sister, Julia, had died. A table, two chairs, and a bed filled most of the small room. Holmes put one of the chairs in a corner of the room and sat down. His eyes travelled round and round, and up and down, seeing every part of the room.

"When that bell rings, who answers it?" he asked. He pointed to a thick bell rope which hung down beside the bed. The end of it was lying on the bed.

"It goes to the servant's room."

"It looks newer than the other things?"

"Yes, it was only put there two years ago."

"Your sister asked for it, I suppose?"

12

"No, I am sure she never used it. We get what we want for ourselves. There isn't often a servant in the house."

"Then it doesn't seem necessary to have a bell."

Holmes walked over to the bed, and spent some time staring at it. Then he took the bell rope in his hand and pulled it.

"Why, it isn't a real bell!" he said.

"Won't it ring?"

"No, it isn't even joined to anything. This is very interesting – you can see it is held to the wall by a nail, just above where the little opening of the ventilator is."

"But how silly! I've never noticed that before."

"Very strange!" said Holmes quietly. "Also, what a strange thing to put a ventilator that goes into another room, and not to the fresh air outside!"

"That is also quite new."

"Done about the same time as the bell rope?"

"Yes, there were several little changes made about that time."

We moved on and went into Dr Roylott's room. It was plainly furnished, but larger than the other rooms. There was a round table and a comfortable chair, and a large iron chest against a wall. Holmes walked slowly around and around, and examined everything with great interest.

"What's in here?" he asked, touching the chest.

"My stepfather's papers."

"Oh! You have seen inside, then?"

"Only once. Some years ago. I remember it was full of papers."

"There isn't a cat in it, for example?"

"No. What a strange idea!"

"Well, look at this!" He pointed to a small bowl of milk which was on top of it.

"There are plenty of animals about, but they are too big to use such a small bowl."

"You said there is a snake in the house·... I think I have seen enough now, Miss Stoner. With your permission, we'll walk in the garden again."

Chapter 10

We left the doctor's room. I have seldom seen my friend Holmes's face so serious or his eyes so angry. We walked for several moments before he spoke to Miss Stoner.

"It is very necessary that you should follow my advice exactly. The matter is so serious that your life may depend on your obeying me completely."

"I will do everything you say."

"Now. Firstly, both my friend Watson and I must spend the night in your room."

Miss Stoner and I looked at him astonished.

"Yes, we must. Let me explain. I believe there is a village inn quite close?"

"Yes, there's the Crown."

"Good. And your windows can be seen from the Crown?"

"Certainly."

"You must go to your room early and not see your stepfather. When you hear him go to bed, you must open your window, and put a lighted lamp at it, as a sign to us. Then you must leave the room, and go to your own room which you used to occupy."

"But what will you do?"

"We shall spend the night in your sister's room, and we shall listen and hope to hear the noise which frightened you so much."

"I believe that you have guessed the answer already."

14

"Perhaps I have."

"Then, please, please tell me how my sister died."

"I must be sure before I tell you anything."

"Will you tell me, then, if you think she died of fright?"

"No, I don't think so. And now, Miss Stoner, we must go. If Dr Roylott returned here and saw us, it would spoil our plans. Goodbye, and be brave. If you do what I have told you, you may be certain that we shall soon drive away the danger, and that you will be safe for ever."

Sherlock Holmes and I got a room at the Crown Inn. It was upstairs on the first floor, and we could see the Stoke Moran house quite easily.

"Do you know, Watson, I am afraid there will be some danger."

"You speak of danger," I said. "You have seen more in those rooms than I was able to do."

"Well, I knew we should find a ventilator before we even came to the house."

"My dear Holmes!"

"Oh, yes, I did. Do you remember Helen Stoner saying that her sister could smell the smoke of Dr Roylott's cigarettes?"

"But is that important?"

"Don't you think it's curious?" Holmes asked me. "Think of the dates. A ventilator is made, a bell rope is hung, and a lady who sleeps in the bed dies."

"I still cannot see clearly."

"Did you notice the bed was nailed to the floor? The lady could not move her bed. It must stay there, near the bell rope, and under the ventilator."

"Holmes," I cried, "I am beginning to understand! We are only just in time to stop another murder."

"Yes, and we have a terrible night to face first."

Chapter 11

All was dark at the house we were watching. The hours passed slowly away, and then suddenly, just as the church clock was striking eleven o'clock, a single bright light shone out right in front of us.

"That is our sign," said Holmes, springing to his feet. "It comes from the right window."

We reached the garden and walked quietly through it, and climbed into the bedroom through the window.

When we were inside, we shut the window and moved the lamp on to the table. Holmes looked around the room. It looked just the same as before. He whispered to me, "We must make no noise."

I showed him that I had heard.

"We must sit without a light. He would see it through the ventilator."

I showed my agreement again.

"Don't go to sleep; your life is in danger. Have your pistol ready. I will sit on the bed and you on the chair."

I took out my pistol and put it on the corner of the table.

Holmes had brought a long thin stick, and he placed it on the bed beside him – with a box of matches. Then he put out the light and we were left in darkness.

Chapter 12

How shall I ever forgot those terrible hours?

I could not hear breathing and yet I knew Holmes sat near, with open eyes, listening and watching, as anxious as I was. It was quite black – not the faintest light shone.

From outside we heard the occasional cry of a night bird, and far away the church clock striking every quarter of an hour. How long they seemed, those quarters! Twelve o'clock – one – two and three, and still we sat waiting silently for whatever might happen.

Suddenly there was a light showing through the ventilator. There was a gentle sound of movement, and then a very small sound, like steam escaping from a pot. As soon as he heard it, Holmes sprang from the bed, struck a match, and beat wildly with his stick.

"You see it, Watson?" he called. "You see it?"

I saw nothing. I heard a low clear whistle. But I could see that Holmes's face was deadly pale and filled with terror and hate.

I reached for the lamp and lit it. Holmes stopped still and looked at the ventilator. Suddenly there was the most terrible cry I have ever heard. It grew louder and louder, pain and fear and anger was in it. It struck cold in our hearts to hear it.

At last it died away and there was silence.

"What can it mean?" I whispered.

"It means that it is all over," Holmes answered. "And perhaps, after all, it is the best thing that could happen. Take your pistol. We must go into Dr Roylott's room."

We took the lamp and entered the doctor's room. I had my pistol ready to fire. There was a lighted lamp on the table. The iron chest was open. The doctor sat on a chair. His head was up and his eyes were fixed in a terrible stare. Round his head there was a yellow band with brown spots. He did not move as we came in the room.

"The band! The speckled band!" whispered Holmes.

I took a step forward. At once the band moved, and I saw it was a snake.

Holmes cried, "The most dangerous snake in India! The swamp adder! In ten seconds after being bitten, he must have died."

As the snake moved towards us I shot it through the

17

Holmes beats wildly with his stick at the speckled band

head. I was shaking at the sight of it. The sound of the shot seemed to wake us from a terrible dream.

Chapter 13

The terrified girl heard the noise of the shot and called to us for help. Holmes calmed her, telling her it was all over, and that there was no more danger for her. He told her his story.

"I knew that the danger was in the ventilator and the bell rope – something was to come through the ventilator and the rope was there to guide that something down to the bed."

"The snake! You knew about the snake?"

"Yes. This kind of poisonous snake has a bite which would not be discovered. This clever and cruel man made use of his Indian knowledge to kill. The snake had learned to obey the whistle you heard, and returned to its master and was given the bowl of milk.

"It was easy to put it through the ventilator, at a chosen time. He was sure it would climb down the rope and land on the bed, and it would bite the person there as soon as he or she moved.

"He kept the snake in the iron chest. The noise of metal falling that you heard was the chest being shut.

"I heard the sound *Sssss* as the snake came through the ventilator and knew that I was right.

"I attacked it with my stick and drove it back through the ventilator. Beating it made it angry, so it went straight back and bit the doctor.

"So I suppose I killed the doctor, but I can't say that I have any feeling of sorrow in my heart!" said Holmes.

Such are the true facts of the death of Dr Roylott and the end of my story.

The Five Orange Pips

Chapter 1

Elias Openshaw sat at the breakfast table. A letter lay in front of his plate.

"From India!" he said, as he picked it up. "Pondicherry postmark! What can this be?"

He opened the letter and out fell five little seeds – orange pips. A strange thing – and the young man sitting with him at the table laughed. But his laugh died at the sight of his uncle's face.

Elias Openshaw's mouth fell open. His eyes stared and his skin turned pale. He held the letter in a shaking hand.

"K K K!" he howled, and then: "My God, my God, I have been found out. What shall I do?"

"What is it, uncle?" the young man cried.

"Death!" said Elias. He rose from the table and left the room, leaving John Openshaw puzzled and very much afraid.

He picked up the letter. The letter K was there three times, and nothing else except the five dried orange pips. What had caused so much terror?

John left the breakfast table. As he was going upstairs, he met his uncle coming down. He had a large key in one hand, and a small black box in the other.

"They may do what they like, but I will win in the end," he said angrily. "Tell Mary" – she was his servant – "that I want her to light a fire in my room today, and send for Fordham, my lawyer."

John had lived with his uncle since he was twelve years old.

Elias Openshaw had come back to England in 1870 after living in America for most of his life. At the time of the American Civil War (1861–65), he fought with Jackson's army.

After the war he settled in Florida, but after making a large amount of money there, he decided to return to England. He bought a comfortable house, with land, in a small town called Horsham. He had no family, so he begged his brother, John's father, to let John come and live with him. He was very kind to the boy, and by the time he was sixteen, John was almost completely in charge of the house. He kept all the keys, did the accounts, and could go where he liked and do what he liked. Elias seemed to like being alone for most of the day.

But there was one room where John was not allowed to go. It was kept locked, and Elias had the key.

With a boy's curiosity John looked through the keyhole on many occasions, but was never able to see more than a collection of old boxes.

Chapter 2

John obeyed Elias and sent for the lawyer. When Fordham arrived, they both went up to the room where Elias had been all morning.

The fire was burning brightly, and all around it there were black remains of burnt paper. The small box that John had seen his uncle carrying stood open and empty.

As John looked at the box, he noticed on it, in large letters, the three Ks which he had read on the letter at breakfast time.

"Fordham," Elias said, "I want you to sit down and

prepare my will. Here are some notes. They will show you who must have my money and other possessions when I die."

While Fordham was writing the will, Elias spoke to John. "I am leaving everything to my brother, your father. In time, no doubt, he will leave it all to you. If you can enjoy my money in peace, that is good! If you find you cannot, take my advice, and leave everything to your worst enemy. I don't know what is going to happen ... Please sign the paper where Mr Fordham shows you."

John signed the will and the lawyer took it away.

This strange event puzzled John. He did not understand his uncle's words, but there seemed to be a dark cloud hanging over the house.

As the weeks passed, John thought less and less about the matter. Nothing happened to change their lives and they continued to live their usual quiet life.

Then John saw a change in his uncle. He started to drink a lot and every day he shut himself away in his room, not wanting to see anyone. One day he came out of his room in a wild state. He rushed round the garden with a gun in his hand, shouting out that he was afraid of no man.

"Why should I live in a prison like a dog chained up. No one can frighten me."

Then, suddenly frightened, he rushed back into the house, and into his room, locking himself in again.

Chapter 3

One night John heard a cry. He got up out of his bed and ran to his uncle's room. The door was open, the room empty. John rushed downstairs and found the door leading to the garden was wide open.

John went to wake a servant and, taking a light, they

went out to search for Elias Openshaw.

They found him at the far end of the garden, face downwards, in a very small lake. There was no sign of a struggle, and the water was only two feet deep. He was dead. Because he had behaved so strangely for the past months, the police supposed that he killed himself.

John was not satisfied. He knew his uncle so well. He knew how he feared death, and he could not believe that Elias would seek it in such a way. But there was no proof that anyone else had killed him. Except for the strange event of the orange pips at the breakfast table, there had been no signs that he had an enemy.

And so the matter ended, and John's father, according to the will, now possessed the house and money that Elias had left when he died. Both he and John decided to live in the house.

When his father first came to the house, John asked him to make a careful examination of the room which had always been kept locked.

They found the small box there. It was empty, except for a paper with the three Ks written on it, and the words "Letters and Receipts" written beneath them.

"Those letters and receipts," John told his father, "must be the ones that Uncle destroyed."

Chapter 4

John and his father were happy for a year. Then once again at the breakfast table, John heard a sharp cry of surprise. His father was sitting with a newly opened letter in his hand. Five orange pips lay on his plate.

He had always laughed at John's story of Elias and the five orange pips, but now he looked puzzled and even frightened.

"What on earth does this mean, John?" he whispered. John's heart felt heavy.

"It's the K K K," he said.

"So the letter says. Here are the letters K K K. It also tells me to put the papers on the stone seat. What papers? What stone seat?"

John said, "The stone seat in the garden. There is no other. But the papers must be the ones that Elias destroyed."

"Well, it's nonsense," said his father, his courage coming back to him. "We don't have that sort of thing happening in England ... Where does it come from?"

John looked at the postmark. "From Dundee in Scotland," he said.

"Why should they write to me about stone seats and papers? I shall take no notice of such a silly letter," said his father.

"You must speak to the police," said John.

"And be laughed at? No. I can't do that."

"Then let me go."

"No, I forbid you. I don't want anything done." John knew it was useless to say any more, but he was very worried about the letter.

Three days later his father decided to go and visit a friend who lived a few miles away. John was glad about this: he thought his father would be safer away from home for a few days.

But he was wrong. He was away for two days, and then John got a message asking him to come at once. He went to the friend's house.

The friend told him sadly, "Your father has fallen over the edge of a high cliff. I found him lying there, but he died without being able to tell me anything."

24

Chapter 5

John was quite sure that his father's death was not an accident.

He went to the place his father had fallen from. There were no signs of a struggle, no footmarks, and nothing had been stolen from the pockets of the dead man. No one had seen any stranger about. And yet John was not satisfied. He was certain that someone had been the cause of his father's death.

Now he was the one to own the house that had once belonged to Elias and then to his father.

Why didn't he leave it, sell it and go and live somewhere far away and escape from this terrible fate that was slowly coming nearer to him?

"No," said John to himself. "I don't think it's possible to get away. It's all because of something that Elias did during his lifetime, and the danger is there, wherever I live."

So he continued to live in the same house for nearly three years.

He was quite happy, and sometimes forgot altogether the strange way in which his uncle and his father had died. He even began to think that the curse on the family was ended.

He was wrong. One morning he opened a letter, and five orange pips fell out.

"Now I *must* go to the police," he thought. "Something must be done this time."

But then he had a better idea. He remembered hearing a friend talk about a detective. This wonderful man never failed to find the wrongdoer he went looking for. John went at once to his friend.

"Ah yes! You mean Sherlock Holmes."

The friend looked at John with curiosity, but John said no more to him. As soon as he had the address, he hurried to London as fast as he could go.

Chapter 6

Sherlock Holmes and Dr Watson were spending a quiet evening together. Dr Watson's wife was away from home on a visit, and he was once again staying with his friend in the house in Baker Street for a few days.

"Was that the door bell?" Watson asked. "Who would be visiting you so late? Some friend of yours, perhaps?"

"I have no friends, except for you," said Holmes.

"Someone wanting your help, then."

"If so, it must be a serious case, to make somebody come here so late."

There was a step in the passage and a knock at the door.

Holmes put out a long arm to turn the lamp away from himself and towards the chair on which the newcomer would sit.

"Come in!" he said.

And as you will have guessed, the man who came into the room was John.

Holmes and Watson saw he was a good-looking young man of perhaps twenty-two. He looked about him anxiously, and they could see that his face was pale and his eyes tired, like those of a man who is filled with some great anxiety.

"I must ask you to forgive me for visiting you so late."

"You have come far?"

"Yes, from Horsham. I have come for advice."

"That is easily got."

"And help."

"Ah – that is not always so easy."

Holmes and Watson at home at Baker Street

"I have heard of you, Mr Holmes, and a friend has sent me to you. He says that you never fail ..."

"He said too much."

"... and that you are never beaten."

"I have been beaten – three times by men and once by a woman."

"But thousands of successes!"

"Well, it is true that sometimes I am successful."

"Then I hope you'll succeed with me!"

Holmes said, "Please draw your chair up to the fire, and tell me, if you can, all I need to know."

"It is no ordinary case," said John. He wondered if Holmes would laugh at him.

"None of those which come to me are. People usually come to me last of all – perhaps even when the police have failed. Now tell me everything that you can, and then I shall ask you about the things that seem to me to be the most important."

Chapter 7

John told them the story from the beginning. The orange pips, the strange K K K letters sent to Elias and his father – everything that you already know about.

Then he took from his pocket the letter that had arrived that day and put it with the five orange pips on the table in front of Holmes.

"You will see that the postmark is London," he said.

"What have you done?" asked Holmes.

"Nothing."

"Nothing?"

"To tell the truth," said John, "I feel helpless. There is some evil coming near to me, and I have no way of stopping it. I am cursed." He let his face fall into his thin white hands and was silent.

"Don't do that!" cried Sherlock Holmes. "You must be a man. Don't give up."

John shook his head. "You don't understand at all."

Sherlock Holmes sat silent for a minute, then he said, "Why did you come to me? And why didn't you come at once? You should have come in the beginning. But now, have you anything – any papers of your uncle's that might be of use?"

"There is one thing," said John. He showed Holmes a piece of paper burnt at the edges. "I found this among the burnt papers in my uncle's room. It seems to be a note. It is my uncle's writing."

Holmes moved the lamp, and he and Watson leaned over the paper. It was headed *March 1869*, and beneath was written:

> *fourth   Hudson came.*
> *fifth   Sent the pips to Paramore and Swain.*
> *ninth   Paramore cleared.*
> *tenth   Visited Swain.*
> *Success.*

"Thank you," said Holmes as he gave the paper back to John. "And now, we haven't got time even to talk over what you have told me. You must go home at once and act."

"What shall I do?"

"There is only one thing to do. It must be done at once. You must put this piece of paper that you've shown us into the black box. You must also put in a note to say that all the other papers were burned by your uncle. Then put the box on the stone seat. Do you understand?"

"Yes, yes."

"We must first remove the danger that you are in. Then secondly we must clear up the mystery, and punish the guilty ones."

"Thank you," said John. "You have given me fresh life and hope. I shall certainly do as you advise."

"Don't waste any time – and above all things, take care of yourself. I am sure that you are in real danger. How will you go home?"

"By train from Waterloo Station."

"Remember to guard yourself well."

"I'm armed."

"Good. Tomorrow I shall set to work on your case."

"I shall see you at Horsham, then?" said John.

"No. Your secret hides in London. It is there that I shall look for it."

"Then I shall call on you in a day, or in two days, with news of the box and papers." And with those words, John left them.

Sherlock Holmes sat for some time in silence, with his head down, and his eyes on the fire. Then he lit his pipe.

Chapter 8

"I think, Watson," he said at last, "that of all our cases, this is the most puzzling."

"Well, yes," said Watson. "John Openshaw seems to be walking amongst great dangers, and yet we cannot say what these dangers are. Who is this K K K and why does he hate this unhappy family?"

"First of all," said Holmes, "we may guess that Elias Openshaw had some very strong reason for leaving America. Men of his age do not change their way of life, or willingly leave the warm weather of Florida for the life in an English town."

Holmes and Watson discuss the puzzling case

"And," said Watson, "his wish to be left alone in England seems to point to the fact that he was in fear of someone or something."

"Did you note the postmarks of those letters?"

Watson said, "The first was from Pondicherry, the second from Dundee, and the third was from London."

"And what does that mean?"

"They are all sea ports. Probably the writer was on a ship."

"Excellent, my dear Watson. That is a good start. In the case of Pondicherry, seven weeks passed between Elias getting the letter and being killed. In Dundee it was only three or four days. What does that mean?"

"A greater distance to travel, but the letter also had a greater distance to come, so I do not see the point."

"Well, I think the explanation of that is: the letter came by steamship, but a sailing ship, taking a much longer time, brought the killer."

"It's possible," said Watson.

"More than that," said Holmes. "It's probable. And now you see the danger that John Openshaw is in. This letter comes from London and therefore we can't expect any delay."

"Oh!" cried Watson. "What can it mean, this endless killing?"

"The papers Elias Openshaw had with him are of great importance to the person or persons in the sailing ship. I think that it is quite clear that there are two or three people, and they mean to get the papers back."

"So the letters K K K may belong to more than one person?"

"Have you never ..." said Sherlock Holmes, leaning forward, talking in a low voice ... "Have you never heard of the Ku Klux Klan, Watson?"

"No, never," Watson replied.

"It was started in America after the Civil War. It was a band of evildoers who went about killing people and bringing terror to any person who did not do what the Ku Klux Klan wanted. To anyone who made them angry, they sent a warning, and from then on he wasn't safe anywhere: his death was certain. Their way of working was so perfect, that it seems they were always successful in their terrible deeds. The American government couldn't end the years of terror until 1869."

"Yes," said Watson, "and 1869 was the year before Elias Openshaw came to England. He brought with him, in the black box, papers that will be the cause of great fear among guilty men. The burnt piece of paper we have seen, with its dates and names of when and to whom the orange pips were sent, are a great danger to the person who has it."

Holmes said, "We can do no more tonight. I believe that the only chance that Openshaw has is to do what I have told him."

Chapter 9

The next morning the sun was shining, and Sherlock Holmes was at breakfast when Watson joined him.

As Watson waited for his breakfast, he picked up the unopened newspaper from the table.

"Holmes," he cried as he opened it, "we are too late."

"Ah!" Holmes said, putting down his cup. "I was afraid of that. How was it done?"

He spoke calmly, but Watson could see that he was deeply hurt.

Watson read out: "A policeman on duty near Waterloo Bridge heard a cry for help and heard someone fall into the river. The alarm was raised, and people passing by gave help, but nothing could be done. Later a body was taken from the river. A letter found in his pocket showed that it was a man named Openshaw,"

They sat in silence.

"That hurts me, Watson," Holmes said at last. "It really hurts me. That young man came to me for help, and I sent him away to his death! Now if God wishes it, I shall destroy these killers, if necessary with my own hands!"

He sprang from his chair, and walked up and down the room. His face was red.

"They must be devils," he said. "Well, Watson, we shall see who will win in the end. I am going out now!"

Chapter 10

Watson did not see Holmes again until the evening.

When he came in, Holmes brought an orange. He tore it to pieces, then he took out the pips and put them on the table.

He put five of them in a letter. He sealed it and addressed it to:

Captain James Calhoun
Sailing Ship "Lone Star"
Savannah
Georgia
America

"That will wait for him until he arrives," he said. "It may give him a sleepless night."

"And who is this captain?" Watson asked.

"He is the leader of these devils. I shall get the others too, but he is the first. I have spent all the day at the Port of London, studying the lists of all the ships which were at

Pondicherry on the right date. I picked out the *Lone Star*, which came from America. Then next, I studied the list of ships at Dundee, where I found the *Lone Star* had also called, and last of all I found that the *Lone Star* had arrived at the Port of London last week. But she sailed for Savannah this morning."

"What can you do, then?"

"Oh, I have my eye on them. There are three Americans sailing in the *Lone Star*. I also found out that all three of them were away from the ship last night. They are the killers.

"When they arrive in Savannah, the mail boat will have carried this letter, faster than the *Lone Star* can sail, and a message will be sent to the police of Savannah that these three gentlemen are wanted here on a charge of murder."

Poor Sherlock Holmes! His plans came to nothing. The murderers of John Openshaw never received the orange pips.

He and Watson waited a long time for news of the *Lone Star* of Savannah, but none ever reached them.

They did at last hear that somewhere far out at sea a piece of wood was seen floating with the letters "LS" on it, which is all that anybody will ever know of the fate of the *Lone Star* and of the men who murdered the three Openshaws.

The Crown of Diamonds

Chapter 1

One morning Mr Alexander Holder, head of the Bank of Holder and Stevenson of Threadneedle Street in London, was sitting in his office. A bank officer came to say that a visitor wished to see him.

Mr Holder was surprised to hear the visitor's name: it was a very famous one, known all over the world – one of the highest and most noble names in England.

"Show him in at once," said Mr Holder. "Don't keep him waiting."

The man who came into the room seemed to be in a hurry, and rather anxious.

"Mr Holder!" he said. "I am told that you often lend money."

"The bank will do that to people of honour," said Alexander Holder.

"It is most important that I should have fifty thousand pounds at once."

"Can you leave with me something of value, to keep until you bring back the money?" said Holder.

"Yes. That is what I expected to do. Perhaps you have heard of the Crown of Diamonds?"

"One of the most precious public possessions in the country? Certainly I have."

The visitor opened a case that he carried. Inside there lay the most beautiful piece of jewellery.

"There are thirty-nine huge diamonds," he said. "This

crown is worth double the money I am asking you to lend me, and I will leave it with you."

Mr Holder picked up the crown. He looked doubtfully at the man who gave it to him.

"Ah, you think it is not mine, and I should not offer it to you. Well, I would certainly not do so if I were not sure that I shall be able to ask you for it in four days' time, when I am able to repay you the money. All I ask is that this matter may be kept secret, and that you take care of the crown. There would be great trouble if any harm came to it."

Mr Holder called for his bank officer and ordered him to pay out the fifty thousand pounds in notes.

When his visitor had gone, Alexander Holder looked at the crown, and began to wish that he had not agreed to keep it. But it was too late to change his mind, so he locked it up carefully until he had finished his day's work.

Chapter 2

At the end of the day, he decided that it was not wise to leave it at the bank. He thought he would carry the case with him for the next few days, so that it would always be within his reach at home or at the bank. So he went home to Streatham, carrying the Crown of Diamonds with him.

When he arrived, he took the case upstairs to his private sitting room and locked it safely away.

In the house at Streatham Mr Holder had his son Arthur and a young girl named Mary, who was the daughter of his dead brother. There were two men servants, who did not sleep in the house, and three women servants who had been there for many years.

His son Arthur was the only one in the house who caused Mr Holder any trouble.

"People tell me I have spoiled him," Alexander said to

37

himself. "Perhaps I have. When my wife died he was all I had to love."

Arthur did not want to work in his father's bank. He enjoyed an easy life among rich friends. Watching horse racing was his favourite occupation. His friends were rich, and so he spent more money than his father gave him, and he often owed money.

Sir George Burnwell was the friend whom Arthur saw most of, and he often came to the house at Streatham. He seemed a pleasant fellow, with good looks and nice manners, but Alexander Holder did not trust him.

Mary was the one person in his house who always pleased him. She was sweet, loving and beautiful, and as tender and quiet and gentle as a woman should be.

"I don't know what I would do without her," he was fond of saying.

Arthur loved her and wanted to marry her, but she refused him. Holder often thought if she married his son, he might become a changed character.

Chapter 3

That evening the small family were having coffee in the sitting room. Holder said, "What a day I've had! I've brought home with me a most precious crown. I have to look after it until next week. It's too valuable to leave at the bank, so I must keep it with me for a few days."

"Where have you put it?" asked Arthur.

"In my sitting room upstairs, locked away."

"Well, I hope thieves don't break in tonight," said Arthur.

"May we see it?" said Mary.

"No, you had better not. I want to leave it where it is," answered Holder.

Mary

That night Arthur followed his father to his room.

"Look, father," he said, "can you let me have two hundred pounds?"

"No, I can't," said his father angrily. "I've been far too generous with you in money matters."

"You have been very kind," said Arthur, "but I must have the money, or I won't be able to face my friends again."

"I don't think *that* would matter!"

"All right, but you don't want me to bring shame on your name. I *must* have the money, and if you won't let me have it, I must try to find it somewhere else."

"This is the third time lately that you have asked me. You shall not have another penny," Holder shouted.

Arthur left the room without saying another word. Holder decided to go round the house and make sure that every door and window was locked.

As he came downstairs, he saw Mary at a side window in the hall. She closed it quickly, and Holder noticed that she looked a little anxious, but then she smiled.

He kissed her and went to his bedroom and was soon asleep.

Chapter 4

About two o'clock in the morning, Holder was suddenly awake.

He heard a sound in the house. He listened, but there seemed to be nothing. Then, again, he heard a small noise, footsteps moving about in his sitting room. Quietly he got up and went there.

Then – "Arthur! You thief! How dare you touch the crown!"

Arthur, dressed only in shirt and trousers, was standing

near a light holding the precious crown in his hands. He seemed to be trying to bend it. At his father's words, he dropped it, and turned very pale. Holder picked it up and examined it. One of the gold corners, with three of the diamonds, was not on it. It was missing.

"You evil boy!" shouted Holder fiercely. "You have destroyed it! You have brought shame on me for ever! Where are the jewels you have stolen?"

"Stolen!" cried Arthur.

"Yes, you thief! My own son a thief!" Holder's voice was full of grief.

"But there are none missing, they cannot be missing," Arthur whispered.

"There are three missing. And you know where they are. Must I call you a liar as well as a thief? I saw you, myself, trying to tear off another piece."

Arthur said, "You have called me enough bad names. I won't say another word. I'll leave your house in the morning and you need never see me again."

"You shall leave in the hands of the police!" cried Holder, half mad with grief and anger.

By this time, everyone in the house was awakened by the noise of the angry voices.

Mary was the first to rush into the room, and at the sight of the crown and Arthur's face, she fainted and fell on the floor.

The police were sent for at once. When they arrived, Arthur said to his father, "Do you intend to ask the police to take me away?"

"It is a public matter; the crown belongs to the country. We can't keep it a family matter. The law must act."

"At least," said Arthur, "let me leave the house for five minutes. It would help both of us – please believe me."

41

"Then you could run away, or hide what you have stolen," said Holder. "Tell me what you have done with the diamonds, and I can still save you from dishonour. You have been caught with the crown. You are guilty. But tell me where the diamonds are, and I will forgive you."

"Keep your forgiveness for those who ask for it!"

Holder found it hard to believe that it was his son who spoke to him like this. But all he could do now was to let the police take Arthur.

A search was made at once – of every part of the house, and everyone in it – but nothing was found.

The police were puzzled, and did not know what to do.

"My advice to you, sir," said the officer in charge, "is to go to Mr Sherlock Holmes, who lives in Baker Street. He is a great detective, and this is the sort of case he has often helped the police with."

"Yes. I believe you are right," said poor Holder. "Of course I have heard of him. He is famous. I will do that, early in the morning."

Chapter 5

"Holmes," I said, as I stood looking down the road, "here is a madman coming along. It seems rather sad that he is allowed to come out alone."

My friend rose lazily from his chair and stood looking over my shoulder. It was a bright cold morning. The snow of the day before lay deep on the ground. A man was coming along the road. He was about fifty years old, well dressed in expensive clothes. As my readers will have guessed, it was Alexander Holder. But his behaviour did not suit his looks, for he was running hard, and as he ran he waved his arms up and down, shook his head, and made mad faces.

"What on earth is the matter with him?" I asked.

"I believe he is coming here, my dear Watson," said Holmes, rubbing his hands.

"Here?"

"Ha! Didn't I say so?" As he spoke, the man rushed at our door and pulled at our bell, making a great noise.

A few minutes later he was in the room. There was such a fixed look of grief and sorrow in his eyes that we were filled with pity.

For a time he could not speak.

Sherlock Holmes pushed him down into a chair, and talked to him gently.

"You've come to tell me your story, haven't you?" he said. "You have hurried too fast and have tired yourself. You must rest until you feel better, and I shall be most happy to help you."

The man sat for a minute. Then he passed his handkerchief over his face, and turned towards us.

"No doubt you think I am mad?" he said.

"I see that you have some great trouble," answered Holmes.

"God knows I have! A trouble that is indeed enough to send me mad, so sudden and terrible it was. Public dishonour I am willing to bear, but that is not all – no indeed! And it is not I alone. The most noble in the land will suffer too, unless I can find an answer to this terrible problem."

"Calm yourself, sir," said Holmes, "and let me have a clear explanation of who you are."

And so Mr Holder told Sherlock Holmes his sad story just as you have read it for yourselves.

When he had finished, he said, "My son was taken to the police station this morning, and I have hurried to you to

43

beg you to help me find the answer to this mystery. What shall I do? I have lost my honour, my jewels, and my son in one night. Oh, what shall I do?"

Sherlock Holmes sat silent for some minutes.

Chapter 6

"Do many friends come to your house?" Holmes asked.

"Very few. A friend of my son Arthur, a man named Sir George Burnwell has been several times. No one else, I think."

"Well, do you go out much?"

"Arthur does. Mary and I stay at home."

"That is not usual for a young girl."

"She is a quiet girl. Not so very young. She is twenty-four."

"This matter has hurt her too?"

"Terribly. I think she feels worse than I do."

"Then both of you believe that your son is guilty?"

"I saw him myself, with the crown in his hands."

"I don't think that proves anything. You say the crown was bent?"

"Yes."

"Perhaps he was trying to make it straight again?"

"God bless you! You are trying hard to help him, and me. But it is too difficult. What was he doing there? And if he was not guilty, why didn't he say so?"

"Exactly. And if he was guilty, why didn't he make up a lie? Why did he keep silent? There are several puzzling points about this case. What did the police think about the noise that woke you?"

"They thought it might be Arthur closing his bedroom door."

"That isn't likely. He wouldn't make any noise if he was

44

a thief. The diamonds that have disappeared – what are the police doing about those?"

"They are looking everywhere – under the floors – in the furniture – hoping to find them in the house."

"Have they thought of looking outside the house?"

"Yes. Everywhere. The garden has been examined."

"Now, my dear sir," said Holmes, "don't you see that this matter is not nearly so simple as you and the police think? You suppose that your son came down from his bed, went to your sitting room, found the crown, broke off a piece of it, then went somewhere to hide this piece – so cleverly indeed that no one can find it – and then returned to the room, putting himself in great danger of being discovered. I ask you: do you think this idea has any sense?"

"But what other is there?" cried the banker. "If he isn't guilty, why doesn't he explain?"

"It is our task to find that out," replied Holmes. "So now, if you please, Mr Holder, I should like to go with you to your house in Streatham, and see things for myself."

Holmes asked me to go with them. I was eager to do that because I was very curious to see what Holmes would do. I must say that it sounded to me as if the son, Arthur, was guilty. But I have such faith in Sherlock Holmes's judgement, that I was sure there must be some hope for the boy, and another explanation for the missing diamonds.

Mr Holder was glad to have the small hope that Holmes gave him.

Chapter 7

The house in Streatham, called Fairbank, was a house of good size, set right away from the road. A wide carriageway led from the gate to the house, and on the right side there was a narrow path between two rows of bushes, leading from the road to the kitchen door. Snow covered the garden.

Holmes walked slowly all round the house, across the front, down the small kitchen path, and through the garden to a lane at the back.

Mr Holder took me indoors, where we sat waiting for Holmes.

After a time the door opened and a young lady came in. I don't think I have ever seen such a pale face. Her lips too, had no colour, but her eyes were red with crying. She took no notice of me, but went straight to her uncle.

"You've given orders that Arthur should be set free, haven't you?"

"No, no, Mary. The police must be satisfied that he is not guilty."

"But I'm sure he has done nothing. I know he has done no harm, and I know you'll be sorry for acting without careful thought."

"Why is he silent, then, if he didn't steal the diamonds?"

"Who knows? Perhaps he was very angry because you didn't trust him."

"But I saw him with the crown in his hand!"

"It is so terrible to think of our dear Arthur in prison."

"Mary, until the diamonds are found, I shall not give up. I have brought a gentleman from London to look more deeply into the matter."

"This gentleman?" she asked, looking at me.

"No. His friend. He wishes us to leave him alone. He is in the stable lane now."

"The lane? What can he hope to find there?"

Holmes arrives by carriage at the house in Streatham

Chapter 8

Holmes came into the room.

"I believe you must be Miss Mary Holder. May I ask you one or two questions?"

"Please do, sir, if it may help to clear the puzzle."

"You heard nothing last night?"

"Nothing, until I heard my uncle shouting."

"Did you fasten all the windows?"

"Yes."

"And were they fastened this morning?"

"Yes."

"I think I would like to look at the windows on the ground floor, and then go upstairs to see round there."

Holmes walked quickly from window to window, stopping at the large one which looked from the hall to the stable lane. He opened it and examined the whole of it very carefully.

"Now let's go upstairs," he said at last.

In the banker's sitting room, he went first to the case where the crown was. He looked hard at the lock.

He opened the case and took out the crown. The edge was bent and cracked where the corner was torn away.

"Now, Mr Holder," said Holmes, "will you try to break off the other corner of the crown?"

The banker looked astonished.

"I certainly won't try," he said.

"Then I will." Holmes suddenly tried with all his strength to break the corner off, but with no result.

"I feel it move a little," he said, "but I can't break it although my fingers are very strong. I don't think anyone could. If I did break it, Mr Holder, there would be a noise like a pistol shot. Wouldn't you have heard it? You weren't far away."

48

"I don't know what to think," said Holder.

"Your son had no shoes on when you saw him?"

"No. Just his shirt and trousers."

"Thank you. Well, I think the matter can be cleared up quite easily, if you will help me, Mr Holder. Now, I'll go outside again."

Chapter 9

He went alone, explaining that any extra footmarks might make his task more difficult. When he came back, about an hour later, his feet were heavy with snow, but he had nothing much to say.

"I think I have done all I can here. I shall return home now."

"But the diamonds, Mr Holmes. Where are they?"

"I don't know."

The banker looked miserable. "I shall never see them again!" he cried. "And my son? Can you give me any hope?"

"My opinion has not changed."

"Then what?"

"You must be prepared to let me spend a large amount of money for you. Then if you come and see me at my house tomorrow, I shall be happy to tell you what I have found out."

And Mr Holder had to be satisfied with those words.

I could see that Holmes had made up his mind about the case, but I could only dimly imagine what he was thinking. He would not talk to me about it on our way home.

As soon as we reached Baker Street, he hurried to his room. He appeared again in a few minutes, dressed as a common beggar. With an old coat, his collar turned up, and old shoes, his disguise was perfect.

"I think that this should do. I wish that you could come with me, Watson, but I do not think it would be wise. I hope to be back in a few hours."

I was finishing my tea when he returned. He looked very satisfied, and was swinging an old shoe in his hand. He threw it into a corner, and took a cup of tea.

"I haven't finished yet. I'm going out again in a minute."

"Where to?"

"Oh, the other side of London. I may be late, so don't wait for me."

"Are you having any luck?" I asked, hoping he would tell me something.

"Yes, I think so. I have been back to Streatham, but I didn't go to Fairbank again. It is a most interesting case. I must change back to my own clothes now." And off he went again.

Chapter 10

I don't know what time he came back, as I went to bed long before he returned. When I came in to breakfast in the morning, there he was with a cup of coffee in one hand and the newspaper in the other. He was quite fresh.

Just then our banker came into the room.

He looked very ill and tired.

"I don't know what I have done to deserve this terrible bad luck," he said. "Only two days ago I was a happy man without a care in the world. But not now. Mary has deserted me."

"Deserted you?"

"Yes. Her bed this morning had not been slept in. Her room was empty, and a note was left for me on the hall

50

table." He gave the note to Holmes. Holmes read:

Dear Uncle,

I feel that all your troubles are my fault, and perhaps if I had acted differently, you would have had no trouble. I can't stay in your house with this thought in my mind, so I must leave you for ever. Don't worry about me. My future is provided for. Please don't look for me. In life or death I am

Ever your loving,
Mary

"What can she mean?" asked Holder.

"I don't know, sir, but I think it is a very good thing that she has gone away. I believe that soon you will see the end of your troubles."

"Ha! You say so! Have you heard something?"

"Would you be prepared to pay one thousand pounds for each of the diamonds?" Holmes asked quietly.

"I've brought ten thousand with me."

"No. Three thousand will do, and I would like the money now."

Chapter 11

When the banker had given Holmes the money, the great detective took out of his pocket a little piece of gold with three diamonds in it and put it on the table.

With a cry of joy Holder picked it up.

"You have it! I am saved! I am saved!"

"There is one other thing you owe, Mr Holder," said Holmes rather sharply.

"Owe!" said Holder, feeling for his money again. "Tell me how much, and I will pay it."

"No, not money, and not to me, but to your noble son.

51

He kept silent to save one he loved."

"Then it was not Arthur who took them? Then let us hurry to him at once, and let him know the truth."

"He knows it already. I went to see him. He would not tell me what had happened, so I told him."

"For heaven's sake tell me, then. What is this mystery?"

"First of all, I must tell you something that will hurt you very much. Your Mary and Sir George Burnwell have run away together."

"My Mary? Impossible!"

"It is certain. You and your son did not know the bad character of the man you let into your house. He is a man without heart or goodness. She believed him when he told her that he loved her, as he has told many a poor girl before. She used to see him every evening."

"I cannot, I will not believe it!" cried the banker. His face was pale.

"I must tell you what happened when the diamonds were taken," said Holmes.

"When you went to bed, Mary came to the hall. She opened the big window there, and talked to Sir George Burnwell, who was outside. I saw his footmarks in the snow, and clearly he was there for quite a long time: the snow was pressed down hard. When he heard about the crown from Mary, he ordered her to get it and bring it to him. I'm sure she loves you, but he had a strong power over her. Just then she saw you coming downstairs again, so she closed the window quickly."

Holmes went on. "Your son Arthur went to bed after seeing you, but he didn't sleep, because of his quarrel with you. Then, in the middle of the night he heard someone go quietly past his door. He looked out and was very surprised to see Mary going into your sitting room. He dressed, and waited in the dark, watching.

"When Mary came out of the room carrying the precious crown, he could hardly believe his eyes. He followed her softly. She went downstairs to the hall again, opened the window, and handed the crown to someone outside. Then she closed the window and hurried back to her room."

Sherlock Holmes looked at Holder.

"What could he do?" he asked. "He loved Mary. But he must stop the crime. He rushed down, opened the window and sprang out into the snow, where he could see a figure of a man in the moonlight. It was Sir George Burnwell. He caught him and fought with him, and cut him over the eye. Then the crown broke, and Arthur had it in his hands. He ran back, closed the window and went to your sitting room. He was trying to straighten the crown when you came in and found him there."

"Is it possible?" whispered the banker.

"You made him angry. You called him a thief, when he thought he deserved your thanks, and he decided not to tell you the truth."

"So that was why Mary fainted when she saw the crown!" cried Mr Holder. "Oh! What a blind fool I am! And when Arthur asked to go out for five minutes, he wanted to go and find the missing piece. How cruel I was to him!"

Holmes said, "Of course when I went into the garden, I saw the footprints in the snow. I saw Arthur's footmarks without shoes on. I saw the place where the snow was cut up by the fight, and I saw a few drops of blood, so I knew I was right. Sir George Burnwell's footmarks went to the end of the lane and the blood drops showed too."

"But how did you find out that it was Sir George?"

Chapter 12

"You told me that you did not have many friends who came to your house. I remembered you told me Sir George was the only one. I knew his name. I knew he was a bad man. My guess was right. I went to his house today as a beggar, and asked his servant for some old clothes. What luck! He gave me some shoes, still wet, that his master had thrown out that day. He also told me that Sir George had a cut over his eye. When I took the shoes to Streatham, I found they fitted the footmarks outside the window of the hall.

"Now, I had a difficult task. I had to get the diamonds from him!

"I changed out of my beggar's clothes and then I went to see Sir George. At first he would tell me nothing. But when he saw that I knew everything, he took up a heavy stick and came towards me. I pointed a pistol at his head before he could strike. He decided to be sensible then. I told him that I would give him three thousand pounds as a price for the diamonds, and promised him he would hear no more about the matter.

"Then I went with the good news to your son Arthur, and at last got to bed at two o'clock in the morning. A really hard day's work I think!"

"A day which has saved England from a great public shame," said the banker, and he rose from his chair. "Sir, I can't find the words to thank you. I have heard of your work, but you are indeed a greater detective than people have told me. I must go at once now and ask my dear son to forgive me. As for Mary, my heart is sad, but even you cannot tell me where she is."

"I think we may be sure," said Holmes, "that she is wherever Sir George Burnwell is. And that, poor girl, will be her punishment."

Questions

Questions on each story

The number in brackets after each question shows you which chapter to look at.

The Speckled Band
 1 Who were living in Baker Street? (1)
 2 Why was the lady shaking? (Because . . .) (2)
 3 Why did Dr Roylott go to prison? (3)
 4 Who was Julia? (4)
 5 What smell came into Julia's room? (4)
 6 What two sounds did Helen hear? (5)
. 7 Why did Helen move into the room that had been Julia's? (5)
 8 How did Holmes know that Dr Roylott was unkind to
    Helen? (6)
 9 Who came into Holmes's rooms after Helen went away? (7)
10 What did Holmes look at in the records office? (8)
11 What was unusual about the bell rope? (9)
12 What was unusual about the ventilator? (9)
13 What did the lamp in the window mean? (10)
14 How did Holmes and Watson get into the room? (11)
15 What was the speckled band? (12)
16 Where was it when they first saw it? (12)
17 Why did the snake bite the doctor? (13)

The Five Orange Pips
 1 Where was the letter from? (1)
 2 Which room could John never go into? (1)
 3 What letters did John see on the box? (2)
 4 Where was Elias Openshaw's body? (3)
 5 What must John's father do with the "papers"? (4)
 6 Where was the letter from? (4)
 7 What happened to John's father? (4)
 8 Why did John go to London? (Because . . .) (5)

9 Why did Holmes move the lamp? (6)
10 What did Holmes tell John to put on the stone seat? (7)
11 How, in Holmes's opinion, did the killer travel? (8)
12 What did he think "KKK" might mean? (8)
13 What happened to John Openshaw? (9)
14 What did Holmes put in the letter? (10)
15 What happened to the *Lone Star* and the murderers? (10)

The Crown of Diamonds
 1 How much money did the man want to borrow? (1)
 2 What did he leave with Mr Holder? (1)
 3 Who was Mary? (2)
 4 What did Arthur want to borrow? (3)
 5 What was missing from the crown? (4)
 6 Where did the police officer advise Holder to go? (4)
 7 Where had the police looked for the missing part? (6)
 8 Which window did Holmes examine closely? (8)
 9 What did Holmes try to do to the crown? (8)
10 What was Holmes's disguise? (9)
11 Who left a note for Holder? (10)
12 How much money did Holmes want? (10)
13 Holder owed somebody an apology. Who was it? (11)
14 Mary had run away. Who with? (11)
15 What did the "beggar" get from Sir George Burnwell's servant? (12)
16 Who sold the diamonds to Sherlock Holmes? (12)

Questions on the whole book

These are harder questions. Read the Introduction, and think hard about the questions before you answer them. Some of the questions ask for your opinion, and there is no fixed answer.

1 In *The Speckled Band*, Holmes prevents a murder.
   a Whose murder does he prevent?
   b Who was the person who planned the murder?
   c Who had already been murdered by the same method?
   d What was the method?
   e What was the reason for the murder?
   f What was the punishment for the murderer?

2 "I knew we should find a ventilator before we even came to the house."
   a Who says those words in *The Speckled Band*?
   b How did he know there would be a ventilator?
   c One side of the ventilator was in Julia's room. Where was the other side?
   d What came through the ventilator?
   e Who sent it through the ventilator into Julia's room?
   f Who sent it back through the ventilator from Julia's room?

3 In *The Five Orange Pips*, Holmes fails to prevent a murder.
   a Whose murder did he hope to prevent?
   b There had already been two murders. Who was the first person to be murdered?
   c What was the method of the first murder?
   d Who was the second person to be murdered?
   e What was the method of the second murder?
   f What was the method of the murder Holmes failed to prevent?

4 In *The Five Orange Pips*, Holmes had plans to bring the murderers to justice.
   a Who were the murderers?
   b Where were they?
   c How did Holmes find out who they were? (He went to the Port of London and . . .)
   d Where were the police waiting for the murderers?
   e What happened to the murderers? (Probably they . . .)

5 In *The Crown of Diamonds*, there is no murder. Holmes clears a young man of blame.
   a Who is the young man?
   b Who blames him?
   c What does the person you have named in *b* accuse the young man of?
   d What did he see that made him blame the young man?
   e Who was really to blame?
   f What was the young man trying to do?

6 "And that, poor girl, will be her punishment." (*The Crown of Diamonds*)
   a Who speaks those words?
   b Who is the "girl" referred to?
   c Why must she be punished?
   d What will the punishment be?

New words

character
(1) a person in a story; (2) the special nature of a particular person, causing him or her to behave in his or her own way

deduce
reach an idea as a result of considering known facts and reasoning from them. The idea reached is one's **deduction**.

disguise
changing one's appearance so as not to be recognised

gipsy
a member of a dark-haired race (perhaps of Indian origin), often travelling from place to place, earning money by making baskets, buying and selling horses, playing music, etc

pip
a seed

speckled
covered with small spots of colour

stepfather
one's mother's second husband, who is not one's father

twin
one of two children of the same mother born at the same time

ventilator
an opening to let air into a room

will
a paper saying who must have one's money and other possessions after one's death